HAPPY BIRTHDAY, AVA!

By Lucy Bell

Illustrated by Michael Garton

Written by Lucy Bell
Designed by Tim Palin Creative
Illustrated by Michael Garton

Library of Congress Cataloging-in-Publication Data

Names: Bell, Lucy J., author. | Garton, Michael, illustrator.
Title: Happy birthday, Ava! / by Lucy Bell ; illustrated by Michael Garton.
Description: First edition. | Minneapolis, MN : Sparkhouse Family, 2017. |
    Summary: "Ava's friends get so caught up in thinking about how they want
    to celebrate her birthday that they forget all about her. A prayer about
    friendship helps them start over and have fun."-- Provided by publisher.
Identifiers: LCCN 2016037152 | ISBN 9781506417868 (hardcover)
Subjects: | CYAC: Birthdays--Fiction. | Friendship--Fiction. | Christian
    life--Fiction.
Classification: LCC PZ7.1.B4523 Hap 2017 | DDC [E]--dc23
LC record available at https://lccn.loc.gov/2016037152

First edition published 2017
Printed in United States
22 21 20 19 18 17   1 2 3 4 5 6 7 8

VN0004589; 9781506417868; JAN2017

SPARK
HOUSE
FAMILY
sparkhouse.org

It was a special day. It was Ava's birthday!

I can't wait to spend the day with my friends, thought Ava. She smiled, thinking of the fun they'd have together. They were going to meet at the big rock to celebrate and eat the cake Ava had made. It was going to be wonderful!

Ava's friends were excited too. They loved celebrating birthdays! The morning of Ava's big day, the friends met at the garden to make plans.

"We need to make this the very best birthday party!" said Jo.

"If it were my birthday," said Hal, "I'd want to make a giant daisy chain that wrapped all the way around the village! That's what we should do."

Hal smiled, imagining all the flowers they would pick. They would find every color of daisy and string them together. The daisy chain would loop and loop around every building, every bush, and everybody.

Uri thought about how she'd want to spend the day if it were her birthday.

"We can sing!" Uri chirped.

Uri imagined her friends making instruments, practicing all day, and then performing their masterpiece for a huge crowd.

"Let's take a birthday hike to the top of the mountain!" said Jo. "Climbing is my favorite."

Jo imagined everyone hiking together, carrying their supplies and singing songs. They could have a picnic and watch the clouds go by.

"What if we built a mountain?"
said Rufus. "Or a giant sand castle
so high it reaches the sky! I love
digging in the sand!"

Rufus imagined finding a nice sandy spot by the stream and digging an enormous moat around an even bigger sand castle. The castle would have lots of windows, turrets, and flags made out of twigs and leaves.

As Ava's friends thought of how to have
the biggest and best birthday celebration,
Ava sat by the rock. All by herself.

Where is everyone? she thought.
Did they forget about my birthday?

Ava decided to look for her friends.

She spotted them laughing and playing in the garden. They had forgotten all about her! Ava's lower lip quivered. Her eyes filled with tears. This was a terrible birthday!

Suddenly, Uri spotted Ava on the path.

"Ava!" she called out.

"Happy birthday!" shouted Jo.

The friends ran to greet Ava.

"It doesn't feel very happy," Ava sniffled.

"What's wrong?" Hal said, concerned.

"You forgot about my birthday!"
Ava said as she burst into tears.

The friends thought about all their big
plans: the daisy chain, the beautiful
song, the long hike, the giant sand castle.
They'd thought up wonderful ideas. But
they hadn't thought about Ava.

"Oh, Ava," said Hal, his face drooping, "we got so excited planning things we wanted to do for your party that we forgot about *you*."

"I'm sorry," said Uri.

"Me too," said Rufus.

"We're all sorry," said Jo.

Ava smiled.

"I forgive you," said Ava. "Besides, all I really want for my birthday is to be with my friends. Now let's go eat cake!"

Ava prayed:

"Dear God, thank you for friends who care about me. Help me be a good friend too.

Amen."

"And thank you, God, for Ava!" Jo shouted.

ABOUT THE STORY

Ava's friends get so caught up in thinking about how they want to celebrate her birthday that they forget all about her. A prayer about friendship helps them start over and have fun.

DELIGHT IN READING TOGETHER

As you read the descriptions of each idea, highlight the silliness by asking your child if the friends could really make a giant daisy chain or a life-size sand castle. What silly ideas can you and your little one add?

ABOUT YOUNG CHILDREN AND PATIENCE

The preschool years bring a child's first forays into friendship. This is when children start to develop empathy, compassion, and the ability to see things from another person's perspective. While it takes years for children to fully develop these character traits, this is a great stage to start encouraging them to think of others.

A FAITH TOUCH

Compassion and empathy are central to living out the teachings of Jesus. As your child's faith grows, be sure to help them find ways to practice showing compassion and care to others through their words and actions. And make sure they see you doing the same.

So in everything, do to others what you would have them do to you.

> *Matthew 7:12*

SAY A PRAYER

Share this prayer that Ava says when her friends ask for forgiveness.

Dear God,
Thank you for friends who care about me.
Help me be a good friend too.

Amen.